Room on the Broom

For Natasha, Sabrina and Jasmine – J.D.

First published 2001 by Macmillan Children's Books
This edition published 2019 by Macmillan Children's Books
an imprint of Pan Macmillan
20 New Wharf Road, London N1 9RR
Associated companies throughout the world
www.panmacmillan.com

ISBN: 978-1-5290-1764-9

1 3 5 7 9 8 6 4 2
A CIP catalogue record for this book is available from the British Library.
Printed in China

Room on the Broom

by Julia Donaldson

Illustrated by Axel Scheffler

MACMILLAN
CHILDREN'S BOOKS

The witch had a cat
and a very tall hat,
And long ginger hair
which she wore in a plait.
How the cat purred
and how the witch grinned,
As they sat on their broomstick
and flew through the wind.

But how the witch wailed
and how the cat spat,
When the wind blew so wildly
it blew off the hat.

"Down!" cried the witch,
and they flew to the ground.
They searched for the hat
but no hat could be found.

Then out of the bushes
on thundering paws
There bounded a dog
with the hat in his jaws.

He dropped it politely,
then eagerly said
(As the witch pulled the hat
firmly down on her head),
"I am a dog, as keen as can be.
Is there room on the broom
for a dog like me?"

"Yes!" cried the witch,
and the dog clambered on.
The witch tapped the broomstick and
whoosh! they were gone.

Over the fields and the
        forests they flew.
The dog wagged his tail
        and the stormy wind blew.
The witch laughed aloud
        and held onto her hat,
But away blew the bow
        from her long ginger plait!

Then out from a tree,
  with an ear-splitting shriek,
There flapped a green bird
  with the bow in her beak.
She dropped it politely
  and bent her head low,

"Down!" cried the witch,
  and they flew to the ground.
They searched for the bow
  but no bow could be found.

Then said (as the witch
    tied her plait in a bow),
"I am a bird,
    as green as can be.
Is there room on the broom
    for a bird like me?"

"Yes!" cried the witch,
    so the bird fluttered on.
The witch tapped the broomstick and
    whoosh! they were gone.

Over the reeds and the
　　rivers they flew.
The bird shrieked with glee
　　and the stormy wind blew.
They shot through the sky
　　to the back of beyond.
The witch clutched her bow
　　but let go of her wand.

"Down!" cried the witch,
　　and they flew to the ground.
They searched for the wand
　　but no wand could be found.

Then all of a sudden
    from out of a pond
Leapt a dripping wet frog
    with a dripping wet wand.
He dropped it politely,
    then said with a croak
(As the witch dried the wand
    on a fold of her cloak),
"I am a frog, as clean as can be.
Is there room on the broom
    for a frog like me?"
"Yes!" said the witch, so the frog
    bounded on.

The witch tapped the broomstick and
    whoosh! they were gone.
Over the moors and the
    mountains they flew.
The frog jumped for joy and . . .

. . . THE BROOM SNAPPED IN TWO!

Down fell the cat and the dog
and the frog.
Down they went tumbling
into a bog.

The witch's half-broomstick
flew into a cloud,
And the witch heard a roar
that was scary and loud . . .

"I am a dragon, as mean as can be,
And I'm planning to have WITCH
AND CHIPS for my tea!"
"No!" cried the witch,
    flying higher and higher.
The dragon flew after her,
    breathing out fire.
"Help!" cried the witch,
    flying down to the ground.
She looked all around
    but no help could be found.

The dragon drew nearer and,
    licking his lips,
Said, "Maybe this once
    I'll have witch without chips."

But just as he planned
   to begin on his feast,
From out of a ditch
   rose a horrible beast.
It was tall, dark and sticky,
   and feathered and furred.
It had four frightful heads,
   it had wings like a bird.
And its terrible voice,
   when it started to speak,
Was a yowl and a growl
   and a croak and a shriek.
It dripped and it squelched
   as it strode from the ditch,
And it said to the dragon,
   "Buzz off! –
   THAT'S MY WITCH!"

The dragon drew back
and he started to shake.
"I'm sorry!" he spluttered.
"I made a mistake.
It's nice to have met you,
but now I must fly."
And he spread out his wings
and was off through the sky.

Then down flew the bird
and down jumped the frog.
Down climbed the cat,
and "Phew!" said the dog.
And, "Thank you, oh, thank you!"
the grateful witch cried.
"Without you I'd be
in that dragon's inside."

Then she filled up her cauldron
  and said with a grin,
"Find something, everyone,
  throw something in!"
So the frog found a lily,
  the cat found a cone,
The bird found a twig
  and the dog found a bone.

They threw them all in
and the witch stirred them well,
And while she was stirring
she muttered a spell.
"Iggety, ziggety, zaggety, ZOOM!"

Then out rose . . .

...A TRULY MAGNIFICENT BROOM!

With seats for the witch
    and the cat and the dog,
A nest for the bird and
    a shower for the frog.

"Yes!" cried the witch,
    and they all clambered on.
The witch tapped the broomstick and
    whoosh! they were gone.